MR. MEN
The Christmas Party

Roger Hargreaves

Original concept
Roger Hargreaves

Written and illustrated by
Adam Hargreaves

EGMONT

The Postman delivered a letter to Thimble Cottage.

Do you know who lives there?

Why, it's Little Miss Shy. Although you'd hardly know because she is so shy you barely ever see her.

The letter was an invitation from Mr Happy to his Christmas party.

Part of Little Miss Shy really wanted to go to the party, but part of her was too shy.

She knew that she would walk into the party and blush and knowing that she was going pink would only make her turn even pinker.

Just the thought of it made her blush!

Mr Happy had a great deal to do to get ready for the party.

But he had lots of help.

Mr Strong had been instructed to go out and find a good sized tree.

And he did!

Mr Muddle glued the Christmas lights and plugged in the paper chain.

Mr Greedy made a cake, but it was not so much a Yule log as a Yule tree trunk!

And Little Miss Naughty brought the mistletoe and chased Mr Happy all round the hall trying to kiss him.

Despite all this help, everything was cooked and decorated and laid and hung the day before the party.

Mr Happy went to bed feeling … well, happy.

But Little Miss Shy did not go to bed.

She could not sleep.

What should she do about the party?

She would be sad if she didn't go. But she would blush if she did.

Would she go? Could she go?

What a dilemma!

When she looked out of the window the next morning she could not believe her eyes.

It had snowed.

It had snowed a lot.

More than a lot, it had snowed buckets!

Little Miss Shy breathed a sigh of relief.

The party would have to be cancelled. Nobody would be able to get to the hall.

When Mr Happy saw the snow he did not feel the same, he felt … well, he felt unhappy.

Poor Mr Happy. What a disaster!

He was going to have to ring everyone and tell them the party was off.

He rang Mr Christmas first.

But Mr Christmas had an idea.

One phone call later, he rang Mr Happy back.

"It's all sorted out. I'm going to borrow Father Christmas' sleigh and give everyone a lift to the party!"

Which is just what he did.

He flew here and there, collecting everyone for the party.

Everyone except Mr Tall, whose long legs made short work of the snow drifts.

The last person he collected was Little Miss Shy.

"I can't go in," sighed Little Miss Shy when they reached the hall. "Please take me home."

"But why?" exclaimed Mr Christmas. "You'll have fun and everyone wants to see you."

"But when I go in I'll blush with embarrassment," explained Little Miss Shy.

"I think you will find," said Mr Christmas, "that everyone has got rosy cheeks on as cold a night as this."

And do you know what?

Mr Christmas was right.

Everyone else looked just as pink cheeked as Little Miss Shy.

"Thank you, Mr Christmas," she said.

Mr Silly and his Fantastic Elastic Band came on stage and the party got started.

And what a wonderful party it was.

They ate and drank, and chattered and gossiped and danced and sang all evening long.

And Little Miss Shy joined in and had a fantastic time.

"You're still looking very pink in the face," said Mr Happy. "Are you still feeling shy?"

"Shy?" said Little Miss Shy. "No…"

"… I'm just very hot from all this dancing!
Happy Christmas, Mr Happy!"